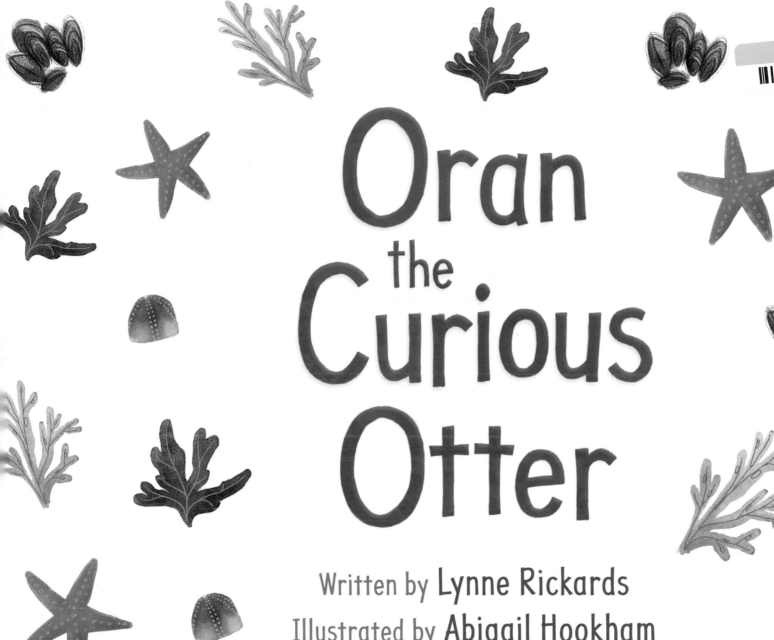

Oran
the
Curious
Otter

Written by **Lynne Rickards**

Illustrated by **Abigail Hookham**

K Picture
Kelpies

Two baby otters were born one spring day
in a holt by a burn near a beautiful bay.

Oran and Orla were tiny and sweet,
but they soon grew much bigger, as both loved to eat.

One morning Mum woke the two pups with a nudge.
They yawned and they stretched but did not want to budge.

"Today is the day that we'll visit the sea.
You'll love it, I promise," said Mum. "Follow me!"

Oran jumped up – he was raring to go!
He was quick and impatient, while Orla was slow.

Both pups followed Mum as she splashed down the burn.
The two little otters had so much to learn.

The water ran down to a wonderful sight:
the sea was so blue and the sand was so white.

The pups stopped and stared at the wide stretch of shore.
They'd never seen anything like it before.

As they came near the sea, Oran got a surprise –
when he jumped in the water, the salt stung his eyes.

"I'm swimming!" he cried, and soon Orla was too.
They circled together as all otters do.

Mum called to the pups, "Look, I've found us a treat.
These rock pools are full of nice shellfish to eat."

The pups started dabbling about with their toes,
when a bold little crab nearly pinched Oran's nose!

"Rock pools are fun, but I want to see more."
So Oran splashed back in the sea to explore.

The view underwater was dappled and green,
with lots of strange creatures and plants to be seen:

Some long, waving seaweed, a school of small fry,
then suddenly something ENORMOUS swam by!

Oran was curious – what could it be?
He raced to catch up, so excited to see…

"Hello, there," he said. "My name's Oran the otter,
and this is my very first time underwater."

"You'll want a wee tour, then," replied the young seal.
"I'll show you around if you like – I'm Camille."

Together they swam to the sandy seabed.
"It's brilliant down here. Look at those!" Camille said.

They watched two big rays and a turtle glide by,
then something unusual caught Oran's eye...

He swam right up close and saw herring inside.
Perhaps he could squeeze through the hole if he tried …

The fish looked so tasty, and not hard to reach.
He'd grab them and have a nice feast on the beach.

Oran reached in with a paw through the gap,
but Camille cried out suddenly, "No! That's a trap!

Don't go any further!" she called. "Oran, wait!
It's meant to catch lobsters, and those fish are bait."

Oran was glad that Camille was so smart.
Not only that, but she had a big heart.

"Since you're so hungry, I'll show you a place
where there's plenty to eat. Come on, Oran – let's race!"

Off they both sped to a rock near the shore.
It was covered in mussels and crayfish galore.

While Oran munched, something blue drifted by.
Might it be some sort of fish he could try?

He swam right up close to it. "Wait!" said Camille.
"Don't eat it," she warned him. "That fish isn't real.

"There are things in the sea that are too hard to chew.
They're all plastic rubbish – they're *not* food for you."

Just at that moment,
two birds fluttered down,
    and Camille ended up with
a black-and-white crown!

The guillemots laughed.
"Hi Camille. Hello, otter.
    We almost mistook you
for rocks in the water!"

"Your mum wants you home," the birds said to Camille.
Her mother had sent them to fetch the young seal.

Oran thought *his* mum might feel the same way.
He'd been out having fun with Camille the whole day!

"Let's meet tomorrow," the two friends agreed.
They splashed their high fives and set off at great speed.

Oran swam back towards Orla and Mum,
who were probably worried he might never come.

After some time, Oran flopped on the shore.
Then down flew the guillemots, laughing no more.

"Camille is in trouble! A fishing net's caught her!
Her flipper's all tangled – she's stuck underwater!"

The birds headed straight for a boat in the bay,
calling to Oran, to show him the way.

The worried birds landed. "Right here," they both cried.
"She's trapped just below us, and now it's high tide!"

Oran took one giant breath and dived down.
He swam like a rocket and looked all around.

Sure enough, there was Camille just below him.
She pointed to one tangled flipper to show him.

Quickly he raced to the net underneath,
and tore at the strands with his sharp little teeth.

He pulled and he twisted. He would not give up.
But could she be saved by a small otter pup?

At last, the net broke – he had set Camille free!
They both struggled up from the depths of the sea.

They swam to the surface for big gulps of air.
"Thanks," Camille gasped. "I'm so glad you were there."

"The guillemots brought me," said Oran. "They knew."
"We make a great team," said the birds, which was true.

Camille said, "My mum will be starting to worry."
Oran agreed, "Mine will too. We should hurry!"

Orla and Mum were as pleased as can be
when *finally* Oran emerged from the sea.

As they splashed up the burn he had plenty to say:
"You'll never *believe* what's happened today!

I met a new friend and she taught me a lot
about plastic and traps, what is safe and what's not."

Mum was amazed when he told her the rest.
Her pup was a hero – the bravest, the best!

Back home in the holt, Oran curled up in bed.
"I'm lucky Camille is my friend now," he said.

Mum smiled and nodded. "Camille's lucky too.
She couldn't have found a friend better than you."